The Last
Polar Bear

Jean Craighead George

PAINTINGS BY Wendell Minor

LAURA GERINGER BOOKS
An Imprint of HarperCollins*Publishers*

To Grandsons Luke and Sam,
who live in polar bear country
—J.C.G.

For Sydney
—W.M.

The artist wishes to thank Thomas Mangelsen for allowing his polar
bear photographs to be used as reference for the paintings in this book.

To find out more about polar bears, visit www.polarbearsinternational.org.

The Last Polar Bear
Text copyright © 2009 by Julie Productions Inc.
Illustrations copyright © 2009 by Wendell Minor
Manufactured in China.

Library of Congress Cataloging-in-Publication Data
George, Jean Craighead, date
    The last polar bear / Jean Craighead George ; paintings by Wendell Minor. — 1st edition.
        p.   cm.
    Summary: Tigluk and his grandmother paddle out into the Arctic Ocean, where they find a young
polar bear whose mother has died because of the changes brought about by the warming climate, and
they bring the cub back to their town so they can teach it how to survive in a changing world.
    ISBN 978-0-06-124067-6 (trade bdg.) — ISBN 978-0-06-124068-3 (lib. bdg.)
    [1. Polar bear—Fiction.   2. Bears—Fiction.   3. Global warming—Fiction.
4. Arctic regions—Fiction.]   I. Minor, Wendell, ill.   II. Title.
PZ7.G2933 Las 2009   2008031419
[E]—dc22   CIP
                                                                                 AC

Typography by Jennifer Rozbruch
09 10 11 12 13 SCP 10 9 8 7 6 5 4 3 2 1
❖
First Edition

Tigluk glanced out the window.
A polar bear was not very far away.

Tigluk put on his boots, wind pants, sealskin
parka, hat, and mittens. As he stepped outside,
a gust of subzero wind stung his cheeks.

He looked down Ivik Street and saw everyone darting into their houses. "*Nanuq!* Bear moving fast! Go home!" a woman yelled as she herded her children inside.

A sudden snow squall blinded Tigluk.
Hearing a noise, he waited.

Crunch,

squeak,

crunch!

Just then the blast of white thinned.

Nanuq was standing right in front of Tigluk. She looked straight at him with her night-black eyes. "What are you trying to say?" asked Tigluk.

Nanuq rose up on her hind feet and flailed her enormous paws. Then she rolled her eyes upward and headed north, as if to say, "Follow me, Tigluk."

Against the white ice she was yellow, then yellow-gray; and finally she was gone, her empty paw tracks appearing one after another.

Tigluk's grandmother came up beside him.

"Nanuq spoke to me," Tigluk said. "I think she wants me to follow her."

"Yes," said his *aka*. "The bear needs you."

"She needs us both, Aka," said Tigluk.

The Arctic had changed that year.
The thaw had come early, fall was staying
longer, and strange trees, flowers, and birds
that usually lived in much warmer places
were appearing. With all the changes in
climate, what would happen to the polar
bears, who needed the ice to survive?

"Aka," Tigluk said, "we must follow
Nanuq together."

The next day Tigluk brushed the snow off his father's old sealskin kayak. The kayak had ripped coming ashore last fall. Aka would mend it. He took it over to her house.

"Can I help?" he asked.

Aka's eyes twinkled. "Mending is a woman's work,"
she said.

"But there is more and more trash in the ocean that
can poke holes in my kayak. It would be good to know
how to mend it," said Tigluk.

"Then I will teach you," she said.

One morning weeks later, Tigluk and his *aka*
paddled into the great Arctic Ocean to find Nanuq.

"Look at those birds," Aka said. "They are guillemots. They never nested so far north before, but now that it's warm, they come here and lay their eggs in old crates and oil drums."

Tigluk and Aka paddled for days, stopping on ice floes and small islands to rest and eat *painiqtaq*, the seal jerky they had sun dried for their journey.

"There are fewer ice floes than there used to be," Aka said. Tigluk knew ice floes were polar bear ships. Nanuq used them to find food and rest.

"What happens if there are no more ice floes?" Tigluk asked.

"Then there will be no more Nanuqs," Aka answered.

They spotted another ice floe. "Look, Aka!" yelled Tigluk. "Those three black spots are Nanuq. They are her eyes and nose!"

Curled on the ice was a very young polar bear cub all alone.

"It's not Nanuq," said Aka, "but her cub. The mother bear must have died or she wouldn't have left her baby unprotected from the gulls." Tigluk got out of the kayak and walked toward the cub. He picked him up.

"I will call him Pilluk, which means to survive. With the melting away of the ice, he is the last polar bear."

"We'll take him back to town and feed him," said Aka.

Tigluk tucked the baby bear in his arms, and the little cub put his arms around Tigluk and licked him on the face.

"Yes," said Tigluk as they paddled toward home.
"Our town will feed Pilluk, the last of the polar bears,
and show him how to live in a warming world."